Transformed

Transformed

BY AMAIA BROOKE

Ruth,
♡ Thanks for your support ♡
♡ you!. Amaia Brooke

Un-Settling Books
Boulder, Colorado USA

Cover Design: Enjoli Izidor
Compositor: Sally Wright Day
Editing: Maggie McReynolds
Author's photo courtesy of Justin Simpson

ISBN: 978-0-578-54197-6

This book is dedicated
to all of the children
who identify as LGBTQ+.
It is meant to inspire you to take flight
and soar higher and higher
into the realization
that you are fabulous
and perfect
exactly as you are.
Dear ones, you are not alone.

Contents

Transformed

x

Chapter 1

Jasper

"**M**r. Morgan, your grandson, Jasper, is in the principal's office waiting to be picked up. He had another incident in class."

Carlisle had called the moment he'd heard the voicemail message. Now he was angry. "Jasper goes by they/them pronouns and doesn't identify as male. How many times do I have to tell them?" he said to himself as he rushed to the elementary school. His beloved grandchild had been bullied during class—again. He was heartbroken that Jasper kept getting mistreated by other kids their age.

The trouble started last year, around the time Jasper had started to grow their hair long and wanting to wear all things pink and glittery. After a time, Jasper had asked Carlisle to use gender neutral (they/them) pronouns when referring to Jasper rather than he/him, and Carlisle had done his best to do so. Every once in a while he slipped up, but he was grateful for the grace period to learn. Other people weren't so accommodating. In fact, some of them had been downright mean. Jasper had just changed schools, and they had hoped it would help.

Carlisle had taken on the role of parent since his daughter, a single mother, had died during childbirth. Sadly, Carlisle's wife, Jasper's grandmother, had died a couple months later from a bad heart. In thirty-five years of marriage they'd only had one child and one grandchild. He was sad that they were both missing out on how special Jasper was. In a lot of ways, Jasper reminded him of his daughter twenty-something years ago, when she'd been the exact same age.

Trying to distract himself, he noticed that the sign in front of the school was covered in leaves. You could barely see the words "Cedar Dale Elementary." Come to think of it, the entire school grounds were messy and overgrown.

"Don't they have people to take care of this place?" he grumbled to himself. He kept glancing at the door. He was getting impatient. He'd made a promise to Jasper after the last time that he wouldn't go inside the school and make a scene. But this meant he was annoyingly stuck in the parking lot and staring at the overgrown hedges.

The door opened, and Jasper and the

principal, Ms. Marx, stepped outside. Jasper met his eyes, and Carlisle could see they looked upset. Their legs shuffled toward him while their pink glitter scarf, still half-wrapped around their neck, blew gently in the wind. Their long blonde hair was still pulled back in a ponytail, now messy from the bully who'd pulled on it.

"Thank you for coming, sir," Ms. Marx said to Carlisle as he approached.

He ignored her and rushed to Jasper's side. He looked down and saw his grandchild's eyes swollen from crying. He bent down and gave them a hug. "Are you okay?" he asked.

Jasper looked up at him with a face full of disappointment. "Grandpa, I'm sorry that you had to come pick me up early," they said sadly.

"You don't need to apologize, kiddo. You did nothing wrong. In fact, I'm proud of you for the way you kept your cool while that kid was saying mean things and pulling your hair," he replied. Carlisle had heard what happened,

4

as well as how Jasper had handled themself in the situation. They didn't fight back, and went immediately to the principal's office, where they knew they were safe.

"Thanks, Grandpa," Jasper whispered. "Can we just go home now?"

The two got in the car, and Jasper started to cry again. "Grandpa, I don't understand why other kids are mean and make fun of me for being different."

"Kiddo, I'm sorry that happened. Sometimes kids can be mean to other kids just because they aren't brave enough to try to understand their differences. If they would look at you the way I do, they'd see the incredible person that I see." Grandpa reached down and wiped their tears away.

Jasper was still sad when they got home, so Carlisle made a fire in the fireplace and two cups of hot cocoa. This had become something of a ritual for the two of them. They curled up together on the couch.

"If your mother were alive, she would be incredibly proud of you," Carlisle said. "Not only for how you handled yourself today, but also because you haven't let those bullies make you afraid to express yourself. You're a lot like her, brave and wise beyond your years." He sipped his cocoa and asked, "Have I ever told you the story about the most beautiful butterfly who ever lived?"

"No, Grandpa."

"Well, I think it's time I do."

Chapter 2

Mikael and Coconut Grove

Long ago and in a land far away, there lived a very special caterpillar who was unlike the rest. His name was Mikael.

Mikael's mother had died saving him from a fire shortly after he was born. Afterward, the island Shaman, a magnificent golden eagle, had watched over him. The Shaman couldn't take in Mikael herself, but she found homes for him with other caterpillars.

Unfortunately, these other caterpillars were often not the best of caregivers. Mikael had ended up bouncing from home to home.

He also got picked on by others his age for being gold—everyone else was green or blue— or for wearing his glitter scarf, or both. The Shaman somehow always knew when things were too unbearable and would swoop in at the right time to rescue him.

Now the Shaman had brought Mikael to a little village called Coconut Grove, located close to the edge of a big and beautiful rainforest on Emerald Island. Many little creatures made their lives in that lovely little place, but it was mainly home to families of green and blue caterpillars. They lived in tiny houses dug into the trunks of giant tropical leaves. Once the caterpillars transformed into either a moth or a butterfly, they could be seen on the tops of the overgrown leaves, flying in the sky, or perched upon palm trees.

As far as anyone knew, there had never been another species of caterpillar in Coconut Grove since the dawn of time. Nothing else had changed there either. Everything was as it always had been, until the Shaman arrived with Mikael.

As Mikael looked around and saw all the other caterpillars staring at him, he started to cry, and tears streamed down his little face.

"Shaman, why have you brought me here? I don't understand. I'm a gold caterpillar, and everyone here is either green or blue." Mikael kicked a rock out of his way in frustration.

"Mikael, I understand that you've had a hard time finding your place in this world because you are not like the others," the Shaman said. "I've told you your whole life there is nothing wrong with being different. Consider yourself lucky. Is there only one color of flower in this world or only one kind of bird?"

"No," Mikael responded. "But why won't you take me to a place with others like me so I can fit in? Everyone is going to make fun of me again." Sick with disappointment, he couldn't meet the Shaman's eyes. Instead, he toyed with the end of his miniature pink glitter scarf, making it glisten in the sunlight.

Jasper interjected, "Grandpa, I wear a pink glitter scarf, and I'm different. I see what you're doing." They looked up at Carlisle, smiling.

Carlisle was happy to see that the events of the day were slowly being forgotten. It was good to see them smiling. "Hey, who's the storyteller here?" he joked. "Just keep listening. Now, where was I? Oh, yes."

"I think this is a good place for you to live for now," the Shaman continued. "I knew your mother, and this village is the place where you were born. She would have wanted you here, especially because you are coming of age now. In a couple of years, you will be able to transform into a butterfly."

They stopped at a tranquil fountain nestled at the edge of the village and close to their destination.

"Your mother loved this fountain. She used to spend a lot of time here," the Shaman said.

Mikael stared at the fountain in awe, looking for any trace of her presence left behind.

The Shaman broke him from his trance. "There is a very mysterious tale about this fountain. It is said that, every so often, it grants a wish when it is made with a pure heart and pure intention."

"When will the next wish be granted?" Mikael asked.

"My family has been keepers of the fountain for many generations, and there is no record of a wish being granted since my family has taken over its care."

"How long has it been?"

"Over a hundred years."

Mikael looked at the Shaman in disbelief. They soon arrived at the door of a tiny home under a giant tropical leaf.

Mikael took a deep breath. "Here we go again," he thought.

Miss Black answered the door. She was an old, dark green caterpillar who had clearly never transitioned to moth or butterfly. "I've been expecting you two since morning. It's evening and about time you showed up," she said abruptly. She went back inside the little house in a huff. "Come inside," she yelled.

Before he followed her inside, Mikael asked the Shaman, "Why is she an old caterpillar? How has she never transformed?"

"It's everyone's choice, Mikael," the Shaman replied. "Some choose to stay caterpillars, and some choose to transform. Sometimes they just want to stay as they are and don't want to change."

"Is that why she's so mean?" Mikael asked.

12

The Shaman didn't reply, but instead turned to leave.

Mikael didn't want to go inside. "Shaman," he blurted.

She turned her beak and focused intensely on Mikael with her piercing eagle eyes.

"I just want my wings so I can fly away and find others like me," he burst out. "You're a powerful Shaman, can't you just use your magic and make me into a butterfly now?"

"No, Mikael. You're not ready. Now isn't the time." She turned, spread her wings, and flew away.

Mikael went inside, head hung low. A single tear dropped down his face, and he immediately wiped it off. Miss Black showed Mikael to his sleeping quarters. Exhausted, he curled up to sleep for the night, but he couldn't stop thinking about leaving. "Miss Black didn't seem too friendly, and this place doesn't seem any different than the others," he thought. He cried himself to sleep.

The next morning, realizing he was stuck in this village, Mikael decided to give his new home a chance. He wanted to visit the fountain that his mother used to love. While on his way toward it, he noticed that everyone was staring at him again. He could hear them whispering:

"Oh wow, check him out. He's gold."

"Look! I've never seen a gold caterpillar before." A green caterpillar pointed at Mikael and fake-whispered to the blue one next to it.

The blue caterpillar came up to Mikael. "Why are you wearing that glitter scarf? Are you a boy or a girl? I thought Miss Black told us she's hosting a boy caterpillar," he said rudely.

The green caterpillar laughed. "Zak, you are funny," he said.

Mikael could feel everyone's eyes on him. Upset, he ran as fast as he could to the fountain and hid there, underneath the shade of a giant tree. He felt sad and alone, but grateful that he was no longer within earshot of the mean things the others were saying about him. "I wish I were invisible," he said to himself.

Mikael gazed into the rainforest next to the fountain and longingly wished he were somewhere else. After a time, he became mesmerized by the steady flow of water and started to relax to its sound. He thought to himself, "I feel like no matter where I go, I don't belong." He looked down at his reflection in the fountain. "I wish others would take the time to get to know me. If they did, they'd see that I'm not really as different as they think I am." He let out a long sigh.

Transformed

Chapter 3

Mikael
and Frankie

Over the next few weeks the fountain became a special place to Mikael. He visited it every day and felt great delight spending time alone, listening to its soothing flow of water. The fountain felt like the only place where he could truly be himself, a place where he wasn't on guard and trying to block out the stares and whispers of others.

He hadn't seen anyone else from the little town of Coconut Grove at the fountain and had begun to think he had the place to himself. But one day, he was interrupted during one of his daydreams when suddenly, out of nowhere, a blue caterpillar ran right into him. He lost his balance and wobbled over onto his back.

"Hey, watch where you're going!" Mikael said, rubbing his head where it had hit the root of the tree. He reached over and gathered his scarf, which had fallen off during the commotion.

"I'm sorry. I had to run and hide anywhere I could." The caterpillar reached out and helped Mikael back onto his feet. "Allow me introduce myself. My name is Francesca. But I hate my name, so just call me Frankie."

"Nice to meet you. I'm Mikael," he replied. "What were you running from?"

Frankie looked over her shoulder and said,

"Three bullies who are really mean to me because I'm different. They pick on me because I like boy stuff and go by a boy name, but I'm a girl."

Mikael inspected her closely. She was wearing a baseball cap on backwards and looked like a boy.

"Have you had any run-ins with the town bully, Zak, and his friends yet?" Frankie asked, breaking him of his stare.

Mikael replied, "If you mean the ones who made fun of me because of my pink glitter scarf when I got here, yes. They haven't stopped bullying me since that day."

"Yep, sounds like them," Frankie said. "Hey, what's with the scarf, anyway?"

Mikael replied, "It was my mother's. She died in a fire shortly after I was born. When I wear it, it feels like she's with me. It makes me feel like I'm not alone." Then, trying not to be overly enthusiastic at the prospect of making a new friend, he asked, "What's with the backwards hat?"

19

"Oh, I feel most like myself when I wear boy stuff," Frankie responded. "It makes me happy."

"My scarf makes me happy too."

Jasper interrupted their grandfather once again. "How do caterpillars wear scarves and hats, Grandpa?" they asked, laughing.

"Anything is possible if we believe," Grandpa responded. "You'll have to be patient and listen to this story because I haven't even gotten to the good part yet."

"Sorry, Grandpa. I really like this story."

"Okay, let's continue then. Where was I? Oh yes, Mikael meets Frankie at the fountain."

But Frankie hadn't escaped the bullies after all. Suddenly, Zak and his friends showed up at the fountain.

"Hey Zak, look at what we have here. The two weirdos are friends now," said one of Zak's sidekicks.

"Well, well, if it isn't the weirdos of Coconut Grove … two little pansies," laughed Zak as the other two joined in. He inched himself close to Mikael and Frankie. The other two surrounded them as if they were about to attack.

"Leave us alone," Frankie said.

"Who do you think you are?" Zak said while he motioned his friends to come even closer.

"You heard me! Leave us alone!" Frankie yelled firmly.

The bullies ran away.

"I've never had anyone stand up for me before. That was brave. I hope I can see you again. You're pretty cool," he said sweetly.

"Likewise," Frankie responded, and then she hurried home.

"I might have made my very first friend," Mikael thought to himself.

The next day, Mikael saw Frankie once again at the fountain. This time, she invited Mikael over to her house. When they walked in, her mother said sharply, "Where have you been, Francesca?"

"I was just, uh…"

Her mother interrupted her. "Please don't

make up another excuse. I don't want to hear it. And take that stupid hat off your head."

Frankie stumbled over her words. "I wanted to introduce you to my new friend, Mikael."

Frankie's mother ignored her. "In this house, you're not allowed to wear that thing. When your father gets home, he'll be upset if he sees you wearing that hat."

Frankie looked down at the floor. Just as she was about to slip it off her head and hide it in her little satchel, her father walked through the front door.

He immediately started to yell at her. "Why are you wearing that hat? You're not a boy. What is wrong with you?"

Mikael felt really sad for his friend and said, "I should go." He walked out the door.

Frankie started to cry and followed him outside, where they hugged.

Mikael turned around to leave. As he was leaving, he heard Frankie's mother yell, "Get back in here, Francesca! Your father isn't finished scolding you!"

Chapter 4

The Fountain

Weeks passed, and Mikael still wasn't fitting into his home in Coconut Grove. He had, however, developed a close friendship with Frankie. They had become the best of friends. And she was the only good thing in his life.

One morning, as Mikael was leaving for the day, Miss Black blocked his way. "Take off that horrible scarf before you leave," she ordered. "If you're living under my roof, then you have to abide by my rules. You're not allowed to wear that thing anymore."

Mikael ran out the door with his scarf still on, ignoring Miss Black's demand. He ran to the fountain, where he sat and cried, "If only I knew where the Shaman lived, then I could find her and ask for her help to find a new home. I don't know why she hasn't shown up yet. She usually comes when it gets this bad. I don't want to live here anymore."

Suddenly, an idea came to mind. He looked at his reflection in the fountain, closed his eyes, and said "Fountain, grant me a wish. Help me find the Shaman so I can ask for her help to find a new home."

Suddenly the water started to swirl, and he could hear a voice speak:

> *At the edge of the rainforest,*
> *across the Raging River*

and on top of the tallest mountain peak:
That is where you will find
the eagle Shaman with the golden beak

He immediately looked around him. "I thought I was alone," he said in disbelief. He then looked into the fountain and saw a picture of a map where the Shaman lived. "Whoa," he said, rubbing his little eyes.

The fountain spoke again:
The time is now right.
You must start your journey before night.
Success isn't achieved solely on one's own.
This journey is far too difficult
to achieve alone.

Just at that moment Frankie arrived. "Are you okay? I've been looking for you everywhere."

"Frankie, the fountain talked to me! I think I just had a wish granted!"

"What? Did you hit your head?"

25

"No, Frankie, I didn't. I asked the fountain to help me find the Shaman so I can get her help to find a new home. It showed me a map where she lives. It also told me that I can't go there alone. Will you come with me?"

"Okay, let me try." Frankie cleared her throat. "Um, hello there, I'm Frankie. Nice to meet you. Uh, where is the Shaman?"

Silence.

Frankie was concerned. "Maybe I should take you to the doctor."

"No, Frankie, I don't need a doctor. It granted me a wish. The Shaman told me that it grants wishes once every hundred years, or something like that. Ask it a question."

"Okay." Frankie looked at the fountain and mumbled disbelievingly, "Where is the Shaman?"

Silence.

Frankie's face filled with worry. "If you won't go to the doctor, then I'm going to take you home to Miss Black."

26

"No, Frankie, I can't go back there. Miss Black told me that I'm not allowed to wear my mother's scarf anymore."

All of a sudden, a voice arose from the fountain:

Do not be dismayed
if you find yourself on a detour.
For you must travel
all four cardinal directions
before you can arrive
at the Shaman's door.

"See, I told you that I wasn't making it up," Mikael said, as Frankie's jaw dropped open in disbelief.

Frankie jumped over to inspect the fountain. "What? There is no way!" She cleared her throat and asked another question. "What is my future?"

Silence.

The fountain started to swirl again and then showed Frankie the map to the Shaman's house.

27

Frankie continued to inspect the fountain. "There must be a speaker or something."

But the fountain stopped swirling and returned to normal, leaving them sitting before it in awe.

"I just don't understand. What is my future? Why won't you answer me?" Frankie begged.

Mikael tried to get Frankie to focus. "Frankie, the fountain was clear. I can't do this alone. I need your help."

"Okay, but I'm still trying to figure out how it did that."

"Frankie, this is serious. I need to find the Shaman to help me find a new home. I can't live here anymore. You must feel the same way. Will you please come with me?"

Frankie sighed. "Mikael, you're right. Every day, my parents yell at me. They want me to be girly. Something I'm not."

"I've never gone on a journey by myself," Mikael said nervously and then recited everything the fountain had said:

At the edge of the rainforest,
across the Raging River,
on top of the tallest mountain peak:
That is where you will find
the eagle Shaman with the golden beak.
The time is now right.
You must start your journey
before night.
Success won't be achieved solely
on one's own.
The journey is far too difficult
to achieve alone.
Do not be dismayed
if you find yourself on a detour.
For you must travel
all four cardinal directions
before you can arrive
at the Shaman's door.

A look of determination came over Frankie's face. "Okay, let's do it. I want a new home too."

Mikael sighed with relief. "Thanks, Frankie."

"Let's get organized," Frankie said. "Grab everything you can and meet me back here in an hour."

"An hour?" Mikael questioned. "How are we both going to get back here in an hour? Miss Black and your parents will never let us leave."

"The fountain said that we must start our journey before night. We're half a day's journey to the edge of the rainforest. If we're going to do this, we must listen to that magic speaking fountain thingy, Mikael."

Mikael considered this. "It must want us to camp at the edge of the rainforest for the night before we cross the Raging River. We better hurry before it gets too late. Let's go get ready."

With that, Mikael made his way back home.

"Where have you been?" demanded Miss Black as soon as he walked in the door. She didn't wait for his response. "I have a list of chores for you to do."

"I have to get going," he responded.

Miss Black wasn't interested. "Your chores come before anything else. I don't care if the Mayor of Coconut Grove invited you to tea. That is that. You've been gone most of the morning."

"But…but…"

"No buts," Miss Black said matter-of-factly.

Mikael froze. "The fountain said we must start the journey before night," he thought to himself. "It's past midday. If I do all my chores, I'll never get out of here before the sun sets. I won't have time to meet Frankie at the fountain to start the journey to the Shaman, and then I'll be stuck here forever."

Determined, he went to his sleeping quarters, packed his satchel as fast as possible, and then jumped out of the window. He'd done it! But just as he landed on the ground, he realized that his scarf must have fallen off while he was packing. He immediately crawled back inside. There was no way he was going to allow Miss Black the pleasure of having it.

While he was retrieving his beloved scarf, he heard Miss Black coming down the hall. She was getting closer and closer, and he was terrified. He started shaking. Before she could reach him, he jumped out the window again and ran to the fountain. He'd escaped!

Chapter 5

The Journey Begins

When Mikael got to the fountain, he found Frankie waiting for him.

"What took you so long?" she asked, annoyed.

"Miss Black wasn't going to let me leave unless I did all my chores. I jumped out my window, and I barely escaped! I have no idea how we're going to make it to the edge of the rainforest before nightfall." Mikael saw that Frankie had been crying. "Did you say goodbye to your parents?"

"No way. They would never have let me leave. I just grabbed what I needed and ran out of there."

She avoided Mikael's eyes and changed the subject. "Hey, I made a map to the Shaman's house while I was waiting for you. It's the same one from the fountain."

She pulled it out of her satchel. It was drawn on top of a dried leaf and rolled up perfectly. She unrolled it and said, "Luckily, Coconut Grove is close enough to the edge of the rainforest that we don't have too far to walk."

Mikael studied the map for a moment. "You drew it perfectly, it looks great! Let's hurry before Miss Black and your parents come find us."

Frankie rolled the map back up, gathered her belongings, and stuffed it all in her satchel. She looked at the path ahead. "I've never actually been past the fountain. I don't know what's out there," she said nervously.

Mikael said gently, "Let's go find out."

They both took a deep breath and inched forward. They had only taken a few steps when Zak and his sidekicks jumped out from behind some bushes and blocked their way forward. "Hey there, where do you think you're going?" he sneered.

Frankie froze.

From somewhere deep within, Mikael found his voice and yelled, "None of your business!"

"Oh, you think you are so brave, little pansy?" Zak laughed, and his friends joined in. "Let me tell you who's boss in this town."

Mikael ignored him, grabbing Frankie and brushing by them, unfazed. "You can have your town because we are leaving," he said. "Also, I really like pansies. They're my favorite flower."

Frankie's jaw dropped open as they walked away.

"Well—well—you think you are all big and important now, but just wait and see! I'll keep you from finding the Shaman!" Zak yelled after them.

Mikael just kept going, Frankie close behind him. "How does he know that we're going to look for the Shaman?" she asked.

"I have no idea," Mikael said. "Maybe he was watching when the fountain granted my wish. Anyway, we don't have time to worry about it now. Let's just keep moving forward." Mikael was determined to leave Coconut Grove.

The light around them faded the further they walked into the rainforest. Mikael looked around. "Frankie, why is it getting so dark in here?"

Frankie looked up. "All I can see are trees. Maybe that's why it's dark."

They both raised their eyes, mentally tracing the giant trees. The tops of them seemed miles away. They were so big that it was impossible to see the sky.

Suddenly, the path ahead of them was illuminated by dozens of little lights. The lights flitted all around the trees and then came closer and closer. Before they knew it, the lights were dancing all around them.

"Frankie, what is that?" Mikael asked.

"Fireflies," she said.

"Wow."

They stared in amazement, fascinated by the tiny lights flying around them. "They're so beautiful," Mikael breathed.

Then they heard, "Ribbit, ribbit, hello there. Oscar the frog here." They jumped and turned around, startled to see a frog behind them.

Frankie grabbed Mikael. "Do frogs eat us?" she whispered in his ear.

"Say, where are you two going? I don't see caterpillars in these parts very often," Oscar said.

Frankie whispered, "Stranger danger."

Mikael whispered, "This journey can't be completed alone. We need help."

Oscar interrupted, "My family has been living in this rainforest for many generations. I can help you find anything."

"We were sent on a journey with a riddle to find the Shaman," Mikael said and recited:

At the edge of the rainforest,
across the Raging River,
on top of the tallest mountain peak:
That is where you will find
the eagle Shaman with the golden beak.

"Riddles only come from the fountain. This must be an important journey you two are on," Oscar said. "I can give you a ride to the edge of the rainforest, next to the Raging River. I will call my friend over to help." He whistled, and another frog hopped over to them. "This is my friend, Clyde."

Mikael and Frankie looked at each other in disbelief while Oscar fastened ropes made of grass around first his, and then Clyde's neck. He whistled for the two caterpillars to hop on.

Mikael jumped on Oscar's back.

"Hold on tight," Oscar said as he started hopping.

"Woohoo," Frankie exclaimed from Clyde's back. "This is so much fun!"

"So, where are you guys coming from?" Oscar asked.

"Coconut Grove," Mikael replied while grasping the rope tightly.

"Oh, I should've known that because that's where the magic fountain is."

Frankie said, "Well, if it's a magic fountain, why wouldn't it tell me my future?"

Oscar chuckled. "Well, it looks like it sent you on an epic journey to find the Shaman, so maybe that question was already answered for you. So, Mikael, what exactly did you ask it?"

"I asked to find the Shaman, to get her help to find a new home. I don't have a family and the Shaman usually finds me homes when things get really tough. She usually swoops in and rescues me from bad places and moves me to the next. The most recent home I was placed in, the lady was mean to me, and I was getting bullied by the other caterpillars my age. The

Shaman never showed up, so now I'm on my way to find her."

"Every hundred years, the fountain answers, but only those with a pure heart, and then only those with a pure intention," Oscar mused. "It must have deemed you very special to have granted your wish."

Frankie interrupted, "What about me?"

"It deemed you very special as well. I'd also guess you weren't fitting in either, were you?"

Frankie and Mikael looked at each other in amazement.

"How could he know that?" Frankie said to Mikael.

They hopped along until they reached what appeared to be the end of the trail.

Oscar said, "Okay, this is the edge of the rainforest. I think we just saved you a lot of time on your journey. There are many obstacles that you will face along the path, but the biggest one is overcoming the obstacles that live deep within yourselves. It's time for me and Clyde to make our way back home. You can make camp here for the night and figure out how you are going to cross the Raging River in the morning."

"Thank you," Mikael and Frankie said. His comments were confusing, but they were grateful for the help.

"You're welcome," Oscar and Clyde replied. They said goodbye, and then they hopped away, back into the rainforest.

Transformed

Chapter 6

Raging River

Frankie stared at up at the dusky sky as the sun finished setting. "It's incredible that we made it here before dark!" she exclaimed.

"I agree, it's pretty incredible," Mikael said.

They felt rain hitting their heads and sought shelter in an empty turtle shell nearby. They ran inside just in time before a downpour. They made their beds for the night and started winding down from the day's journey.

After some thought, Mikael said, "If we keep getting help like we did from Oscar and Clyde, then I think everything is going to be okay."

"To be honest," Frankie said, "I'm kind of scared. I don't know what to expect. The only thing that I know is Coconut Grove. What if we find animals who try to eat us?"

Mikael thought for a moment. "What if they all help us like Oscar and Clyde did? What if we find the Shaman and get a new home? It's better than staying in Coconut Grove."

A giant crack of thunder erupted, and a flash of lightning illuminated the entire night sky. The thunder kept rolling, followed by heavier rain. The storm was so abrupt that they stopped talking for a moment.

Mikael continued, "Honestly, I don't know why others treat me so bad just because I'm different."

44

"I feel the exact same way, Mikael," Frankie replied. "I don't quite understand either. Everyone, including my family, has made me feel weird my whole life for not being like them. You're the only person who's made me feel like I'm normal just as I am. You're my best friend. I don't know what I'd do without you."

"I don't know what I'd do without you either, Frankie. You're my best friend too."

The rain slowed down and gently lulled them to sleep.

The next morning, the sun rose, the birds chirped, and the only evidence left behind of the storm was its memory. They sat in front of the abandoned turtle shell in the sunshine, eating fresh leaves and thinking about the day's journey ahead. They were close to the Raging River and could see it in the near distance. They still hadn't figured out how to cross it.

Out of nowhere, they heard, "Squawk, squawk!" Above, a seagull, a glint in its eye and its beak open, started diving toward them.

45

Frankie exclaimed with alarm, "I don't think this one is going to help us!"

They got up and ran as fast as they could into the abandoned turtle shell and blocked the opening with some rocks they found inside. Luckily, the shell was small enough that the bird couldn't fit into it.

The seagull seemed dumbfounded. It looked around for its prey, inspecting the turtle shell, and poking through the openings with its beak. Then it flew away, defeated.

Mikael said, "That bird was definitely looking for its breakfast."

They were relieved it was gone.

Frankie took out the map and inspected it closely. "The fountain said we need to cross the Raging River to find the Shaman. Maybe we need to build a boat?"

Mikael considered this. "No, let's walk to the river's edge. I have a feeling there'll be something waiting to help us. This whole journey started with the fountain granting my wish and telling us we can't do it alone. Maybe we'll find help to get across."

They packed up their things and got underway. As they walked along the shoreline, looking for a way to cross the river, Frankie noticed something moving behind her. She whipped around, but there was nothing there but leaves. She kept going and saw movement out of the corner of her eye again. It looked like the leaves had moved from one place to another on the trail. She stopped abruptly in her tracks, hoping to catch them in motion. Still nothing.

Mikael was focused on the task at hand, how to cross the river, and didn't notice anything.

Frankie heard a noise and looked up. She saw the seagull flying above them. She yelled, "Mikael, the bird is back!

They heard, "Squawk, squawk!"

Frankie started to inch forward quickly, but smacked into the leaves that had suddenly

47

moved right in front of her path. She looked around, startled. "Hey, wait a minute! Those weren't there a second ago."

Frankie and Mikael were both staring at the sky now, and the bird started diving toward them. They ducked, not knowing what to do.

All of a sudden two of the leaves jumped on top of them and covered them protectively.

The bird was dumbfounded and looked everywhere for the prey that he'd just seen. He soon gave up and flew away.

As soon as the bird was gone, the two leaves uncovered them.

Frankie said, "Wow, you're walking leaves! I didn't know such a thing existed." She inspected them very closely. The leaves were twice their size and had eyes and antennas. Their bright green bodies were standing on eight legs and looked like dried leaves broken into perfect parts, like two puzzle pieces that could have fit together nicely.

One of them spoke. "My name is Lola,

and this is my brother, Sawyer. We've been following you since you were on the trail in the rainforest. We were lost and were trying to find our way back home to the Raging River. We didn't know how to make our way out of the rainforest and overheard you tell the frog that you have a map. So, we followed you out."

Frankie's eyes grew wide. "You're walking food!" Her jaw was open, and she was drooling.

"Please don't eat us. We are not really leaves; we are bugs just like you," Sawyer said. "We only look like leaves so we can protect ourselves from predators."

Mikael said, "It's a pleasure to meet you. Thank you for saving us from the bird." He reached out and wiped the drool off Frankie's face.

"We've never met a caterpillar before," Lola said shyly. "We usually stay away from your kind for fear that you might try to take a bite."

"You wouldn't like the taste if you were to bite down," Sawyer said nervously.

They all laughed with relief that no one was going to get eaten. Then they heard footsteps approaching and began to quiet down.

"Well, well, well, looks like one big, happy group of inspiration here." Zak and his sidekicks appeared.

Lola let out a scream.

Mikael noticed the river was calm where they were standing. He looked at Zak and then over to his two new friends. "Can you swim?"

"Yes," they responded.

Mikael eyed the water. "You think you can swim us across?"

Frankie chimed in. "It's only a short distance to the other side."

In response, Lola and Sawyer jumped into the river. Their bodies looked like two leaves floating alone on the water. "You two jump on, and we'll carry you across," Sawyer said.

Mikael and Frankie looked at each other, held hands, and jumped into the river. Frankie climbed onto Lola's back and Mikael, onto

Sawyer's back. Lola and Sawyer started swimming hurriedly to get away.

Zak yelled out from the other side, "You got away again, but I will find you, and I will hurt you both!"

Mikael felt a little scared, but when he looked over at Frankie, he saw that she had a giant smile on her face.

"This is so much fun!" Frankie stood tall on Lola, pretending that she was surfing. "I can't believe we are in the water!"

After they made their way across, Frankie and Mikael thanked Lola and Sawyer for their help.

Lola said, "Thank you for getting to know us instead of eating us. I think you'll find the same kindness along your journey."

They said goodbye to their new friends and set off toward the tallest mountain peak.

Transformed

Chapter 7

Detours

"We made our way across the Raging River. Now how are we going to get to the top of the tallest mountain peak?" Frankie asked as she sat down and began chomping on a leaf.

"No idea, but I imagine we'll find help,"

Mikael replied, sitting down next to her. He had found a leaf to eat too.

Frankie pulled out the map. "There are only three tall mountains on the island, and they're all right next to each other. The one in the middle is the tallest of the three." She put the map down, looked up, and pointed out the middle one, still far away. "It looks like it will take us forever to get there, Mikael. We aren't going to be able to do it ourselves, at least not without wings."

"I guess we should start making our way toward it."

They packed up their things and started inching forward. As they approached a meadow, they spotted a deer. Its head was down, and it was eating grass. As they drew closer, the deer lifted its head and looked straight at them. "It's a beautiful day to be on such an important journey," it said.

Frankie was confused. "H-how did you know that we were…"

"My name is Dawn," she interrupted. "I take it you are Frankie."

"Um, yeah."

Dawn looked over at Mikael. "And you must be Mikael."

He smiled and nodded his head.

She said, "I am going to take you to the owl. She will help you to continue on the rest of your journey to find the Shaman."

At this point, Mikael didn't even question it. When Dawn approached them and bent her head so they could climb on, Mikael shuffled his little body onto her neck and nestled in.

Frankie didn't move. She was standing on the ground in protest and refusing to climb aboard. "How did you know who we are and that we were on a journey to find the Shaman?" she demanded.

Dawn chuckled and responded, "The entire island knows that you are on the journey to find the Shaman because the fountain granted you a wish to find her. It hasn't granted a wish in a hundred years."

Frankie let down her guard and climbed onto Dawn's neck. Once Frankie was settled next to Mikael, Dawn began walking.

Frankie gazed at Mikael, wide-eyed. "The whole island knows?"

Mikael didn't answer. Instead, he asked the deer, "Who is the owl, and how is she going to help us find the Shaman?"

"The owl knows the Shaman, and she will tell you how to find her."

"Where does the owl live?" Frankie asked. "Hey, we're going to the wrong mountain!" She took out her map in a panic.

"The owl lives at the base of the second largest mountain on the island. Do not be discouraged. This is an important detour. She is a wise creature. You won't be able to find the Shaman without her help."

Mikael reminded Frankie, "'Do not be dismayed if you find yourself on a detour, for you must travel all four cardinal directions before you can arrive at the Shaman's door.'"

Frankie put the map back in her satchel.

Dawn gave a nod of approval. "Okay, we must hurry now. Hold on tight, and I will run there."

They held on tight while the deer ran to the owl's house. Eventually, they arrived at a giant tree at the base of the mountain.

"This is where she lives," the deer said as she looked up to the top of the tree. "She lives at the top, but she sleeps during the day and is awake at night. Since it is now midday, it might be wise to wait to climb up and find her."

Frankie and Mikael thanked Dawn for her help.

She replied, "It was my pleasure." She started to leave, but then turned back and said, "The detour you are about to embark on is the most important part of your journey."

She turned around and left.

As they rested on the trunk of the owl's tree, Mikael looked around for some food. "Frankie, we should eat, and then try to climb up there. I don't want to wait."

"That's a good idea. I'm famished. This detour is taking up enough time as it is. I don't want to wait either," she replied.

They found some big, juicy leaves and sat down to eat, looking up at the tree.

"I am pretty sure this is the biggest tree I've ever seen in my entire life. How the heck are we going to climb this thing?" Frankie asked.

"I don't know," Mikael replied.

They finished their meal and started to pack up their satchels, readying themselves to climb up the tree.

An owl swooped nearby. Frankie cried out, "Danger, danger! Look, an owl! Quick, run for cover!"

Mikael was mildly annoyed. "We're here to see the owl, remember?"

In one swoop, the owl scooped them up in her beak and took them far up into the tree. She sat them down on one of the branches.

"Who, who are you two, trespassing on my property?" the owl hooted in an authoritative tone.

"We are on a journey to find the Shaman and were told that you could help," Mikael said.

Frankie was shaking. While keeping her eyes locked intensely on the owl, she whispered to Mikael, "She's pretty scary. I'm not so sure about this detour."

"Oh yes, I have been expecting you two." The owl's voice softened. "Mikael and Frankie, right?"

Mikael nodded his head.

Frankie grimaced.

"Nice to meet you both. My name is Nona." She looked over at Frankie. "You can relax. I won't eat you."

Frankie relaxed.

"It is being said that the fountain granted you a wish, to find the Shaman. Is that true?"

They nodded.

"I know the Shaman well. I've worked alongside her for many years, and she has been a great teacher to me. You will need to bring her five gifts in order to get her to help you to find a new home. You will travel all four cardinal directions, to all the keepers of the sacred gift elements that the Shaman cherishes greatly. Once you have done this, you will then be guided to the fifth and final place, Fairy Island. The fairies are the keepers of the Sacred Crystal, which is the most sacred gift for the Shaman and the hardest one to obtain. Many have attempted to bring this gift to the Shaman, and many have failed. Once you gather all of them, you will then be taken to the Shaman."

"This is quite a detour," Frankie said. "And it sounds complicated. I thought you were going to show us the way, not just give us tasks and instructions. How long is this going to take, anyway?"

"You will have help along the way to get to each place quickly. Remember, you must bring the Shaman these gifts in order to get her help," Nona replied.

Mikael and Frankie looked at each other, overwhelmed.

"The Shaman has swooped in and helped me find homes my whole life. Why all of a sudden do I have to bring her gifts in order to get her to help me now?" Mikael asked.

"Even though you had a wish granted from the magic fountain to find her, you are still running away from your home. You must face that which you are running from, the reason you left in the first place, before she will help you. The most important part of your journey is ahead of you right now because of this."

Mikael looked discouraged.

Nona continued. "First, you will travel to the east to visit King Muno. He is a great king and keeper of the Sacred Fire. We must hurry to make it there before sunset, and then you will stay the night in his kingdom. But before we leave, I must tell you the story of the phoenix."

Frankie was impatient to get going, but she settled herself next to Mikael to listen.

Mikael rested his head on Frankie and readied himself.

"There was once a great bird who was tortured by deep darkness. The darkness brought upon him great hardships, many of which made the bird very sad and angry. No matter what the bird tried, he could not alone conquer the darkness that had befallen him. Desperate for help, he heard of a great king who would help heal him of the darkness that tortured him. That king was the keeper of the Sacred Fire."

Their eyes were widened.

"That sounds scary," Frankie commented.

Mikael asked, "King Muno?"

Nona continued without answering. "He had heard that this fire would burn away all the darkness that had plagued him. He went on a long journey to find the great king, and finally, after much searching, succeeded."

"Um, is that where we're going?" Mikael asked.

"Am I the only one who is terrified here?" Frankie asked.

"The great King and keeper of the Sacred

Fire told the bird to surrender to the fire and allow the fire to consume him. When he surrendered to the fire, he was then withered into nothing more than ashes. After time passed, he began to rebuild himself better and stronger than before, without any darkness and with pure light, thus becoming the great phoenix. He became the greatest bird who ever lived."

Mikael and Frankie's eyes were big, and their jaws were wide open in silence.

"Your story is like that of the phoenix. You must navigate through the darkness that plagues you both and overcome it. This will be the most challenging part of your journey, but if you stay on the path and don't give up, you, too, will transform like the phoenix."

Frankie said, "Wait a minute. That was a great story, and I don't want to speak for my friend here, but I don't want to be consumed by a fire. Count me out of this." She made as if to leave the branch and head down the trunk of the tree.

"A Sacred Fire is not a real fire," the owl said gently. "It is a light that illuminates the dark parts of us in order to help us heal.

Frankie paused to listen.

The owl continued, "The shadow parts of ourselves can be our medicine, if we let them."

"What are my shadow parts?" Mikael asked.

"We all have different things or experiences that cause pain, and we call these our shadows, our inner darkness. The Sacred Fire will help you see what yours is, so that you can expose it to the light and burn it away."

Mikael questioned Frankie. "Are you really going to leave? We've come so far! And the owl said that it isn't a real fire. It's some sort of magic light thing."

Frankie drew herself up. "The owl is right. We've been running away, but we haven't really faced why we left. My parents treated me badly because I like to dress like a boy. Is the pain of that experience my inner darkness?"

"I can't answer that for you, my dear," Nona said. "You will have to visit the Sacred Fire and find out for yourself."

"Okay, let's get out of here then," Frankie said.

The owl replied, "Climb on my back, and I will fly us there."

Transformed

Chapter 8

East–King Muno and the Sacred Fire

They said goodbye to Nona the owl and made their way to the east before sunset. It was getting dark, but soon they found themselves standing at the entrance to the King's forest and contemplating going inside.

Frankie frowned. "We aren't going to be able to see anything in the dark."

Just then, a monkey carrying a torch emerged from the forest and greeted them. "I am King Muno," he said.

They were startled for a moment and gazed up at him. Mikael was particularly mesmerized. He'd never seen a monkey before. He was captivated by the strong character and emotion he could see in the King's facial expressions. Standing upright on his two legs, King Muno looked strong and mighty, yet his face looked gentle and kind. He had wrinkles on the sides of his eyes that made him look old and wise.

The King reached out one of his large hands, palm up, and said, "Come, I will take you to my kingdom. Jump in."

Frankie and Mikael jumped into his hand. As the King made his way down a hill, they noticed a clearing surrounded by banana trees. There were a lot of monkeys sitting around a roaring fire in the center of the clearing. The monkeys all jumped up and down as they got closer—it appeared that this was their way of greeting the newcomers.

Frankie ignored the greeting. "Um, that actually looks like a real fire," she said worriedly.

King Muno sat them down on a rock far away from the fire pit but close enough to still be in the circle of monkeys. He then seated himself on a special rock that appeared to be his alone and said, "I heard you were sent here for a special gift to take to the Shaman. You also seek the medicine of the Sacred Fire?"

"Yes." Their voices trembled.

Mikael said, "We were sent to have the Sacred Fire burn away our darkness."

Frankie interjected, "But I don't want to be consumed by the one we are sitting in front of because that one looks like it will hurt."

The entire monkey forest started laughing and jumped up and down again.

Frankie asked Mikael, "Why is that funny? I was being serious."

"The Sacred Fire is not a real fire," King Muno said. "It is not the one that we are sitting in front of. It is a sacred tool to help us illuminate the darkness within. The darkness is any pain we have experienced in life, or any negative emotion or feeling that blocks us from happiness. It shines the light on the areas that we need to focus on so that we can adjust and alter our inner selves to have happier lives. If you are willing, I will take you there."

They looked at each other, and each let out a long sigh. Mikael said, "Okay, let's go."

The monkeys started jumping up and down again and made strange noises.

King Muno paused to listen. It was as if they were deciding their fate with the Sacred Fire.

King Muno nodded and then picked up his torch with one hand and Frankie and Mikael with the other. "Let us go," he said. He carried them deeper into the rainforest, far away from the firepit and the rest of the monkeys.

Soon, they found themselves being taken

into a cave. It was pitch black, but the path was illuminated by the light of King Muno's torch. As the King made his way deeper into the cave, they could see a faint light ahead that grew brighter and brighter as they neared it.

Mikael shielded his eyes from the glare. Then he looked up and saw the moon and stars in the sky. It seemed almost like they had walked out of the cave, except that he could see the stone walls still surrounding them. They were in some sort of half-cave, half-open space. King Muno had stopped walking and had placed the torch in a special place in the wall that held it nicely. They had reached their destination.

Frankie, shielding her eyes too, said, "This is a weird cave. I've never heard of one that had a hole in the top to see the sky before. Have you, Mikael?"

"No."

They were terrified.

The intensity of the Sacred Fire was strong. Mikael was unsure of what to expect. In the center of the space, the bright light was other-worldly. His eyes began to adjust, and he looked around and saw artwork all over the cave's walls, art that appeared to be from those who had come before them and who had been brave enough to allow the Sacred Fire to consume them.

King Muno sat them down in front of the Sacred Fire. "Now, ask it what you need to know. Ask it what darkness you need to bring to the light."

Frankie was nervous. "Uh, hello there, Mr. or Mrs. Sacred Fire. How do you do on this fine evening?" She looked panicked, trying to figure out how to ask what the King directed.

Mikael sat quietly as if in a trance, staring at the Sacred Fire. He could hear it speak to him but noticed that no one else appeared to hear what it was saying.

"Jump in," the Sacred Fire said to Mikael.

King Muno asked Mikael, "What is the Sacred Fire telling you?"

Mikael was surprised that King Muno knew

that it was speaking to him and responded, "To jump in."

"Then you better jump," the King said firmly.

"But my mother died in a fire. I don't want to die," Mikael said, frightened.

"You must overcome your fear so that you can be free of darkness and be happy. It's not an earthly fire. This is a Sacred Fire." King Muno reached out his hand and stuck it in the fire, holding it there for a long time. "See?" he said while laughing, and then he turned around to leave. Before he left, he turned back and said, "It's only here to help you, if you allow it. There's nothing to be afraid of." He paused for a moment, "You will camp here for the night, and I will take you to your next destination in the morning."

He was gone.

Mikael looked back at the Sacred Fire nervously.

Frankie said, "I'll jump with you."

"Okay."

They took a deep breath, held hands, and then jumped. They noticed there was no sensation of heat, only the intensity of a bright light shone around them. Now, standing in the Sacred Fire, they could both hear it speaking aloud.

They heard, "There is nothing wrong with either of you for being different than other caterpillars. Let my light burn away the idea that there is something wrong with you. Let my light burn away the pain of your elders' or parents' rejection of you, and the pain of others your age telling you that there is something wrong with you for not being like them. You are perfect just as you are."

Frankie started crying. "But my whole life I was told there is something wrong with me because I am different," she said.

Mikael was also crying, and said, "Me too. I bounced from home to home and was rejected for being different. I was also bullied for not fitting in."

"I am telling you that there is nothing wrong with either of you. You must stop believing what others have told you about yourselves. You must believe in yourselves. You must allow my light to burn away the pain of those experiences so you can begin to be happy."

They stood there, eyes closed, and allowed the light to burn away every false idea about themselves they had ever heard, and all the pain of rejection they had ever felt. When they felt complete, they stepped out of the Sacred Fire.

Mikael glowed. "I feel like a weight has been lifted off of me."

"Me too," Frankie replied.

They made their camp for the night next to the Sacred Fire.

They were lying there staring up at the stars. "I was not expecting that at all," Frankie said.

"Me either," Mikael replied. He reflected for a moment "I have to admit it was nice to hear. I always wonder what my mother would say about how different I am. I'd like to think that she would have said the same exact thing. That there is nothing wrong with me."

"I think she would," Frankie smiled.

Soon, they were fast asleep.

The next morning, King Muno arrived at the cave. "Did you get your answers?" he asked. His face said he already knew what had happened after he left.

"Yes, we did," Mikael answered.

"Good! We must now make our way to the south. I am going to take you to the keeper of the Sacred Garden of the Earth. Here is the gift for the Shaman." He pulled out a vial that contained a small portion of the Sacred Fire inside. It was glowing just like it had the night before.

Frankie opened her satchel, and King Muno dropped it inside.

"How does the Sacred Fire fit into that little bottle?" she asked while peering into her newly lit bag in awe.

"We'd better get going," King Muno replied.

He reached down, scooped the two friends up in his hand, and set out on their journey.

Transformed

Chapter 9

South–Marakata and the Sacred Garden of the Earth

King Muno dropped them off in front of a trail and said, "Marakata is the keeper of the Sacred Garden. He is very wise, and you will benefit greatly if you listen to what he has to say." He pointed toward the trail and continued, "Just follow this trail, and you won't be able to miss it. It is the most beautiful garden on the island."

"Thank you so much for showing us the Sacred Fire," Mikael said. "It's incredible to know that there's nothing wrong with me for being different."

"I agree with Mikael," Frankie said. "It's a relief to know that I am perfect just as I am. Thank you, King Muno."

"It was my pleasure to assist you both on such an important journey," King Muno replied. He then headed back to his kingdom.

Mikael and Frankie followed the trail until they arrived at the most beautiful garden they could ever have dreamed of and noticed a praying mantis at the entrance. His bottom legs were crossed, and his hands were in a funny formation. His eyes were closed. He appeared to be meditating.

Keeping his eyes closed, he said to them,

"Oh pray tell, youthful ones, to what do I owe the pleasure of making your acquaintance?"

Frankie waved a little hand over his face, but he didn't flinch. Instead he said, "Hello Frankie, nice to meet you."

"How did you know my name?"

"I know answers to questions before I ask them," he replied. "One does not need their eyes to see. Oh, I really like your hat. It looks very nice on you."

"Whoa, thanks," she replied, impressed.

Keeping his eyes closed, he then changed his focus to Mikael and said, "Nice to meet you too, Mikael. I love the scarf. I have some roses that color of pink in my garden. It looks very lovely on you."

Mikael looked at Frankie in surprise.

"We were sent to ask you for a gift for the Shaman," Frankie said. "Or maybe you already knew that," she added.

"Oh joy! I have been expecting you both. My name is Marakata. I am the keeper of the Sacred Garden of Earth."

His eyes were still closed, and Frankie started to make funny faces to get his attention.

"Frankie, those faces are not attractive on you." He paused and concentrated again.

"I can see that both of you have been mistreated so far in your lives," Marakata continued. "And the Sacred Fire told you that there is nothing wrong with you for being different. I can also see that it has burned away the pain of those experiences. Am I right?"

Mikael and Frankie gave each other a look of disbelief. Mikael said, "Yes."

Frankie whispered, "Whoa, how does he know all of that?"

"We all have a Sacred Garden inside of us," Marakata said. "Did you know that?"

"No," Frankie said.

Mikael shook his head.

"I can see that both of your inner gardens aren't doing so well because they have had unkind things spoken to them. You must have believed the mean things that others have said to you that made you feel like there is something wrong with you," Marakata said matter-of-factly. "Let me tell you about the Sacred Garden of Earth. I walk around each day, and I speak loving things to each of the plants, flowers, and trees. It helps them grow big and strong. Because I do that, it is the most beautiful garden on the island."

Mikael and Frankie took this in solemnly.

"I will take each of you to your own place in the garden to speak love to one of the plants, flowers, or trees. When you are ready and have the hang of it, I will have you close your eyes like me and speak love to yourselves, to your inner gardens. Now I will show you both where to go." Marakata finally opened his big green eyes and walked into the garden.

As they were following him inside, Mikael asked, "Why does my inner garden need work? I'm nice to every creature and treat them with respect. I don't understand."

"Yes, Mikael, but I can see that your inner

83

dialogue to yourself isn't kind," the praying mantis replied. "You have believed the mean things that were said to you by peers or caregivers your whole life. You must love yourself and treat yourself with the same kindness you give to all others."

They stopped in front of a bunch of pansies. Marakata pointed to the flowers and said, "Start by telling these pansies how beautiful they are despite being different than the other flowers."

"It sounds so weird when you say it like that," Mikael said. "All flowers are beautiful, especially pansies."

"Exactly," Marakata replied.

Mikael sat in front of the pansies, looked at them, and said, "You are beautiful despite being different than other flowers."

He stopped and awaited further instruction.

Marakata said, "Good. Now tell them how loved, beautiful, and strong they are. If you have trouble, just picture them as someone or something that you love very much."

Mikael contemplated for a moment and then started speaking loving things to the pansies.

Marakata then focused his attention on Frankie, who appeared to be struggling to understand. "Okay, dear one, now it is your turn." He guided her over to a palm tree. "You don't seem like the flower type of girl."

"Right again," she responded.

"Now tell this palm tree how confident, brave, and special it is."

"You are cool after all," she responded, and she sat down in front of the tree and started talking.

After time passed, and Marakata deemed them ready, he instructed them to speak in the same loving way to their inner gardens. "Tell yourselves, your inner gardens, the same kinds of things you were telling the plants."

Mikael closed his eyes and said to himself, "You are beautiful. You are loved. You are strong."

Frankie closed her eyes and said to herself, "You are confident. You are brave. You are special."

After a short time, gold dust started swirling around them.

Frankie said to Mikael, "Whoa! You're glowing!"

Mikael exclaimed, "So are you!"

"My heart feels like it's smiling," Frankie said.

"So does mine," Mikael replied.

Marakata looked happy. "Good. I think you two got what you needed. Now don't forget you must keep tending to your inner gardens, especially when a negative thought, such as fear, doubt, or discouragement about yourselves, comes to mind." He ushered them both toward the entrance and handed Mikael a small vial. "Here is part of the Sacred Garden of Earth for the Shaman."

Mikael put it in his satchel.

Marakata then handed Frankie a rock. "Here is a rock for you. You will need it later on your journey." She looked at it in confusion but then put it in her satchel.

"I am going to have my friend, Leo the

leopard, take you to the west, to the Sacred Water Temple and the Waterfall of Truth. Marakata made a whistling sound, and Leo appeared. "Please take them to the Sacred Water Temple," the praying mantis told the leopard. "They are ready."

Marakata turned back to Mikael and Frankie and said, "Now you best be on your way. Off you go."

"Thank you, Marakata, for teaching me how to speak love to my inner garden," Mikael said. "Yeah, that was pretty cool. Thank you," Frankie said.

Marakata said goodbye and returned to his garden.

The two friends were left looking up at the leopard. He was a giant cat with big paws and sharp claws. He had a big mouth and even bigger teeth. He looked at them with intense yellow eyes.

"I am confident. I am brave," Frankie said, shaking in fear. She noticed they were standing next to a large body of water and turned to Mikael. "Quick, I've heard that cats hate water. Let's jump in!"

"I won't waste my time eating you. What are your names?" Leo asked, cool and calm.

"My name is Mikael, and this is my best friend, Frankie."

"Nice to meet you both. Hop on, and I will take you to the Sacred Water Temple."

"Um, Mikael, do we trust leopards?" Frankie murmured.

Leo laughed. "Hop on, and I will tell you my story." He bent his head down, and the two friends hopped on.

"I come from deep in the rainforest and have many friends, but my dearest friends are those just like you, the caterpillars," Leo said, moving through the trees. "You see, I was found wandering the rainforest alone as a cub, crying for my mother. I could not find her. I was so hungry that I curled up in a ball and cried myself to sleep. I must have been lying on a caterpillar home. They came out to investigate. They found me lying there and could tell that I was starving and had no mother, so they sent for the Shaman."

"Wow, that was nice of them to help you," Mikael said.

"The Shaman took me into her house and nursed me back to health. When I grew up, I went back to thank them, but they were already gone. They must have transformed into butterflies. So now I thank them by helping everyone that I can. I wouldn't be alive if it weren't for the kindness of those caterpillars."

"I would have never guessed that something as big and scary as you would be grateful for a little family of caterpillars like us," Frankie said, amazed.

They continued to make their way through the rainforest. Soon, they arrived at the Sacred Water Temple, where Leo dropped them off.

"Thank you for your kindness," Mikael said as he waved goodbye.

"Thank you, Leo," Frankie said.

"It was my pleasure to help you two on your journey," Leo replied. He turned around, and the pads of his feet treaded lightly on the ground as he gracefully made his way back into the jungle.

Chapter 10

West–The Sacred Water Temple

Mikael and Frankie found themselves hesitating at the entrance to the Sacred Water Temple, a bit wary of entering. The temple was a big building shaped like a pyramid and surrounded by a gate. The sound of a rushing waterfall could be heard in the near distance.

"Frankie, I know that we swam across the Raging River and made it out okay, but I'm afraid of water," Mikael said, reluctant to inch forward.

Frankie gave him a sympathetic glance.

They started to inch forward and noticed that a dog was sitting at the doorway of the gate. It was wearing sunglasses. They exchanged looks of curiosity.

The dog greeted them as they approached. "My name is Felix."

"I'm Frankie, and this is my best friend, Mikael," Frankie said.

"Nice to meet you. Are you two headed inside to the Sacred Water Temple?" Felix asked.

"This is the entrance, right?" Frankie asked. She inspected him more closely, trying to figure out why he was wearing sunglasses. "Mikael," she whispered, "That dog is a pit bull." She started inching back. "Aren't they supposed to be dangerous?"

"That's precisely why I'm here," Felix said, having apparently overheard Frankie. "Creatures run away from me all the time because we pit bulls have a bad reputation for being mean. I'm not mean at all. I love making new friends." He shook his head sadly. "I've never hurt anything, not even a fly."

"Why are you sitting down here and not inside at the Waterfall of Truth?" Frankie asked.

"Those who see their reflection in the waterfall see themselves as they truly are, they can see their authentic selves. I've been sitting at the entrance for a week, too scared to go inside," Felix said. "I'm scared it will tell me I'm a monster. What will I do then? I'm not a bad dog, and I want to keep it that way."

"But if you're already a good dog, why would it show that you're a bad dog on the inside?" Frankie asked bluntly.

Felix looked down at the ground. He wiped a tear off his face and replied, "You are right, I am a good dog. I guess it's silly to worry that it would show me differently. Can I walk inside with you?"

"Yes!" they responded.

The trio started to make their way inside.

"Why do you wear sunglasses?" Frankie asked.

"Because I want to hide that I'm a pit bull so creatures will stop being afraid of me. We really are a kind breed despite our reputation."

"Well, why would you listen to that if you already know that you are good?" Frankie said, sympathetically. "We were bullied back home in Coconut Grove, and were made to feel like there was something wrong with us by our caregivers and peers. Mikael had a wish granted from the magic fountain, and now we are here. We've made lots of friends who've accepted us for who we are, and we're learning to love and accept ourselves."

"Wow," Felix said, "You two are so wise, and you're not even the size of my paw. How did such incredible wisdom come from something so tiny?" His glasses slid down his nose as he peeked at them in amazement.

For the first time, they could see Felix's eyes. "Wow, you have golden eyes!' Mikael enthused. "They glow and are so beautiful. They are the same color as me! Why don't you take your glasses off so everyone can see your eyes?"

The Waterfall of Truth came into view. The pyramid that they'd seen from the outside of the temple gates was even more magnificent inside. Its golden hue glistened in the sun. Fountains were perfectly placed inside the surrounding water, each flowing in unison. They appeared as tiny streams in comparison to the giant flow of the great waterfall, which flowed from the center of the pyramid. A perfectly built stone walkway was placed underneath the waterfall, and creatures were lined up to see their inner truth in its reflection.

They were standing on a path close to the surrounding water when Mikael noticed a dolphin swimming up to them. "That must be the keeper of the Sacred Water Temple," Mikael said to his companions.

Felix bent his head down to the water, and he and the dolphin spoke for a moment. Then he turned to Frankie and Mikael and said, "I am going to get in line to see my truth at the waterfall. Good luck to you two!"

Frankie and Mikael said goodbye as Felix made his way to the line, then they focused their attention on the dolphin.

"Welcome, welcome," the dolphin said. "My name is Sachi. Jump in! I have been expecting you." She splashed water at them playfully.

They started to laugh and then heard, "Squawk, squawk!" They looked up at the sky.

"Oh no, Frankie, it's that seagull again," Mikael said in a panic.

Sachi said, "Quick, jump in."

They jumped, and Sachi scooped them up so that the bird missed them by barely a second. She swam them over to safety and sat them on a rock close to the waterfall for instruction.

"Now I must tell you about the waterfall before you enter," she said. "It is a magic waterfall that allows you to see your inner true self, or authentic self, in its reflection. What that means is, it is like looking in a mirror, but you will see who you are on the inside rather than the outside. Once you look at it, your reflection staring back at you won't be the version of you that I am looking at right now, it will be your inner truth. Make sense?" she asked.

They nodded.

"Okay," Sachi continued, "You will have to go one at a time and wait for the other to finish before you take your turn. Each of you must respect the other's journey."

They glanced over at what had been the line of creatures they saw when they arrived and noticed it was gone. The only one left was Felix, and he was making his way through.

They glanced back over at Sachi.

"Now, which of you is going first?"

"I am," Frankie said. She made her way over to the walkway under the waterfall and took a deep breath. She inched forward and paused when she had gotten close enough to see a full reflection. She was amazed because it was exactly like Sachi had said. The reflection was her, but not what she looked like at all. Instead it showed an incredible version of herself, and she couldn't help but want to stare at her inner truth for hours and hours. She saw a confident, strong, and brave butterfly looking back at her. It was happy and flying free. She was smiling from ear to ear and then realized Mikael needed to take his turn. Once she made her way through, Sachi was waiting for her at the other side of the walkway in the surrounding water.

They watched Mikael take his turn.

Mikael took a deep breath and inched forward. When he could see his reflection, he was surprised. He was loved, brave, and flying free. He had many friends. But there was something else that was different about him too. He sat there in amazement, unable to speak. He joined Frankie and Sachi with tears in his eyes.

Frankie examined Mikael. "Why are you crying?"

Mikael didn't respond.

Sachi said, "I am proud of both of you for looking at your inner truth. It takes courage to do that. Frankie, what did you see?"

"I saw a confident, brave, and special butterfly."

"Mikael, what did you see?"

"I am not ready to talk about it yet."

Sachi responded, "Okay."

"I need some time to think," Mikael said.

Frankie gazed at him, not knowing what he was going through. She turned to the dolphin and asked, "How can I help?"

Sachi responded, "He'll be okay. Just be there when he's ready to talk. When you are both ready to move on, I will have Felix the dog take you to the north to visit the Sacred Temple of Wind. I must say goodbye. Oh, and here is the gift for the Shaman." She tucked a little vial of Sacred Water into Frankie's satchel with her mouth.

Frankie said goodbye to Sachi as she watched Mikael inch away and sit down by himself, staring at the water. Frankie was worried for her best friend. She paced while he sat there.

Finally, Mikael arose from his perch on the rock that overlooked the beautiful water. "Okay, let's get going."

They made their way back to the gate, where Felix was waiting for them.

His sunglasses were gone, and his golden eyes glowed as he said, "Wow, looks like I am a good dog after all. That was great! What about you two?"

Frankie responded, "It was great for me, but I'm not sure about Mikael. He doesn't want to talk about it yet."

They made their way to the north in silence, on Felix's back.

Chapter 11

North–The Sacred Temple of Wind

Mikael was still silent when they arrived at the Sacred Temple of Wind. They could see a giant tree house surrounded by a clearing of grass, with a small garden next to it. A little stone temple faced true north in the clearing.

Felix dropped them off at the base of the treehouse. They said their goodbyes to their friend. No sooner had he padded off when they were greeted by a parrot. They were intrigued because they'd never seen a parrot up close before. It was incredibly colorful. A green patch on top of its head faded into a blue that covered its neck and spread to half of its body. The other half was purple, including its wings. Its breast was yellow, and a hint of orange highlighted the bottom next to its black feet.

The parrot looked at them, and then opened its black beak and started speaking. "Oh, what do we have here? Oh, wait, I know who you two are. I was told to expect you. Frankie and Mikael, right?"

"Yes," Frankie answered.

The parrot placed one wing on his hip and raised the other expressively. "I am Jade, the keeper of the Sacred Temple of Wind!" he exclaimed in a dramatic tone. He looked down at the two, but there was no response. "Such a captive audience. So, were you told about me or the Temple of Sacred Wind?

"No," Frankie said.

"Oh, that's interesting. Interesting indeed. Okay, well what are your talents then?"

"Talents?" Frankie said confused and slightly irritated. "You aren't going to eat us, are you?"

"Heavens no. I am on a vegetable diet to keep slim." He folded his wings on his waist and preened, then continued, "Tonight is our big show, and we're missing two performers. We have such a short time to rehearse. I was expecting you hours ago!"

Frankie shook her head in bewilderment. "Rehearse?"

"A choir of my bird friends and I sing and dance for the entire island. It's a grand performance," Jade said proudly.

"Oh wow," Frankie said. "Wait a minute, just how many of the birds in your choir are vegetarians like you?"

"We are all vegetarians, we're all watching

our figures, and we always look good," Jade said smugly. He waved a wing in the air. "Look at me. I don't look this fabulous for the audience by eating bugs." He pranced around them.

"Actually, who *is* in your audience?" Frankie asked.

"Was that a joke?" Jade asked. "Have you never heard of our famous show? Wait, are you a comedian?"

"You didn't answer my question."

"Basically, the entire island comes to see it," Jade said while waving his wings around flamboyantly. "Have you really never heard of it?"

"Wait, you do a performance for the entire island?" Frankie asked.

He pointed up at the deck of the treehouse. "We use the deck as the stage, and we sing and dance together. It's the main event of the island, and everybody sits in the clearing to watch it. You and your friend here are going to perform tonight."

"But I'm not a performer. I'm just a young caterpillar," Frankie said in protest.

Jade replied, "You aren't going anywhere with that attitude."

"I'm no performer either." Mikael finally spoke.

"You just came from the Waterfall of Truth, right?" Jade asked.

"Yes," Mikael said, not getting where this was going.

"Then you must have seen your true and magnificent selves, am I right?"

"Yes."

"It is not necessarily a performance. It is about showing your authentic self to the island. Our yearly show is about honoring our authentic selves. Tonight, you should honor yourselves by expressing what you saw at the Waterfall of Truth. Say and do whatever you want up there. Take over the show for all I care. Just show us your true selves."

Mikael froze. "Nobody has ever wanted me to show my true self. Everyone has wanted me to just fit in, my whole life. I have never had anyone believe in me before and give me permission to be myself."

Frankie spoke up. "Me neither. I can show my authentic self?"

"Please do," Jade said. "Now you two better run along and figure out what you are going to do. And, after tonight's performance, I'll give you a gift for the Shaman. You'll camp here for the night and be on your way in the morning."

Mikael and Frankie walked back to the garden, found some leaves that looked extra delicious, and sat down for their meal.

"Maybe I can be a comedian for the night. I guess I can figure out a funny thing to say," Frankie said.

"You always say funny things," Mikael said.

Frankie thought for a moment. "Okay, here's a joke. Knock knock."

"Who's there?" Mikael responded good-naturedly.

"Bug!"

"Bug who?"

"Bug off," Frankie grinned. "I'm a caterpillar trying to become a butterfly!"

Mikael laughed. Frankie looked proud that she had successfully cheered him up.

Mikael quieted. "I saw myself as a beautiful butterfly at the Sacred Water Temple," he blurted out.

Frankie looked carefully at him. "This whole time you've been upset because you saw yourself as a beautiful butterfly?"

"No, Frankie, you don't understand. I saw myself as the most beautiful butterfly who ever lived."

"I don't understand. That sounds amazing!" Frankie frowned in confusion.

"My whole life, I have not just been different for being gold," Mikael explained. "and I don't just wear the pink glitter scarf to be close to my mother. I also like to feel feminine. When I wear it, I feel like me—because inside, I'm a girl."

Frankie's face cleared. "Mikael, you're talking to a girl caterpillar who likes to wear boy clothes and do boy things. I kinda get it, I mean, not entirely, but I love you no matter what."

"Thanks, Frankie."

They hugged.

Mikael said, "Maybe I'll dance with the birds in the performance."

"Hey, you could have Jade dress you up beforehand," Frankie suggested. "You can change the scarf for a feather boa and use some of that color stuff on your eyes. I think you would look so pretty."

"Really? You wouldn't be ashamed of me if I did that?" Mikael asked.

"Are you kidding? I could never be ashamed of you," Frankie said firmly. "Besides, if you are going to become the most beautiful butterfly who ever lived, then I definitely want to stick around and continue to be your cool best friend when you are famous."

Mikael laughed in relief.

Frankie got quiet for a second and then said, "I wasn't completely honest at the Waterfall of Truth. I saw myself marrying a girl butterfly when I saw my true self."

Mikael smiled. "Was I your maid of honor?"

Frankie smiled back. "Absolutely."

They embraced again.

Over Frankie's shoulder, Mikael saw that Jade had lingered to overhear them and was crying. "My eyes can't be puffy for my performance tonight!" he exclaimed. "Luke, Lukey, can you get me that special eye cream, please?" Jade flew off, squawking to his husband.

Mikael looked down. "I'm nervous about showing my true self as a female tonight to everybody on the island though."

Frankie gave him a hug. "I am scared to show my true self as a lesbian tonight." She paused for a moment. "Remember that the Sacred Fire told us that we are perfect just as we are?"

"Oh yeah, it did," Mikael said.

"We also have a new tool to help us to overcome our fear of showing our true selves to the island. Marakata told us that if any doubt, fear, or discouragement about ourselves comes to mind, we should tend to our inner garden. We should speak love to our inner gardens to help us both love ourselves and be brave to show our true selves tonight."

"That's a great idea, Frankie."

"I think we should close our eyes like Marakata showed us," Frankie urged, "And just imagine our own inner gardens."

They sat there in silence, eyes closed, and spoke love to themselves. When they were done, they found Jade and his friends and spent some time rehearsing for their performance that night.

Before the show, Jade made a boa out of feathers for Mikael and put color on his eyes. When it was showtime, Mikael froze with fear. He was reluctant to step out on stage and show his true self to the entire island. He started to shake. He looked over at Frankie, who was flirting with a girl caterpillar in the audience by winking at her. This was his big moment, and he couldn't get Frankie's attention. His heart started to pound in his chest, and he almost tripped over his feather boa. He closed his eyes and said to himself, "I am beautiful and strong. I love myself, and I deserve to be happy." He stepped onto the stage with his eyes closed. He heard a cheer and then opened his eyes and danced with the birds. He was doing it! Surprisingly, he felt wonderful and free— and was gratified when the crowd applauded enthusiastically.

Jade had made a newsboy hat and a bowtie for Frankie. She realized that Mikael had taken his turn, and that now it was her moment. She made sure her bowtie was on straight and took a deep breath. "I am confident, and I am brave," she said to herself. Her heart pounded, and it felt as if it was going to beat out of her chest. Her hands and arms began to shake. She felt as if she was going to pass out. She took a deep breath, took to the stage, and told her joke. The crowd went wild! She had a huge smile on her face as she listened to the audience roar with laughter.

After the show, they camped in the treehouse for the night. They both thought they would never fall asleep, but all the excitement had been a little overwhelming. They had just closed their eyes when before they knew it, it was morning and time to set out for Fairy Island.

They made their goodbyes.

Jade looked at Mikael. "Last night, you were the most beautiful caterpillar that I've ever seen," he said with tears dropping off his beak. "I'm impressed at how fast you learned the dance moves. The crowd loved you! I'm also very proud of you because I could see that you were struggling with your inner truth, but you've been brave and showed it to the world. Thank you for your strength."

Jade turned to Frankie. "And you were wonderful, you funny little comedian. The crowd was floored by you. I'm proud of you, too, and how good you were at helping Mikael when you could see that he was struggling. I'm so happy that you were able to show your whole truth too. Thank you for your courage."

He patted them both on the head and handed Mikael the gift for the Shaman, a vial of Sacred Air. "Ava the elephant is going to take you to Fairy Island so you can get the Sacred Crystal. I am excited for you two to meet my friends, the fairies! They are so adorable. Good luck on your final mission!"

They said goodbye to Jade and his husband Luke, and sat to wait for Ava to take them to Fairy Island.

Transformed

Chapter 12

Fairy Island and the Sacred Lotus

In no time, Ava the elephant appeared at the edge of the clearing. But before she could reach them, the seagull came out of nowhere. It dove straight at them crying, "Squawk,

squawk!" They tried to inch away quickly, but the seagull snatched them up in its beak.

At that same moment, Ava reached out her trunk and made a noise that sounded like a trumpet. She swung her trunk at the seagull's beak, dislodging Mikael and Frankie, who landed neatly on top of the elephant's head.

"Are we alive or dead?" Frankie asked after a long pause.

"That stupid seagull!" Mikael exclaimed as he looked over at Frankie, who still had her eyes shut in fear and was shaking. Mikael reached over and tried to comfort her. "Hey, open your eyes. We're alive."

"Is this heaven?" Frankie asked.

"No, we're still on earth. Open your eyes. The elephant saved us. Did you not see any of what happened?"

"No, I thought we were dying, and I didn't want to see."

"We were saved by Ava," he said.

Frankie opened her eyes and looked around.

Ava asked, "Are you two okay up there?" She motioned with her trunk and tilted her head.

"Yes," Mikael called.

"Oh no! Where's my hat?" Frankie frantically looked around for her beloved hat.

Mikael spotted it on the ground. He slid down Ava's trunk and retrieved it.

Ava picked him up and placed him back on her head, where Mikael handed Frankie her hat.

"Thanks," Frankie said, relieved.

"Are we ready to depart?" Ava asked.

"Yes," Mikael responded.

"Good," replied the elephant. "Now, I hear that we are headed to Fairy Island. Let's get going." She let out another trumpet sound, and off they went.

They walked half the day on the elephant and then arrived at the shore of a beach. They could see Fairy Island in the near distance. Ava stopped walking, and they were greeted by two fairies who appeared as if they had been waiting for them. They were twice the size of Frankie and Mikael. Their bodies looked human, but with wings half their size in the same color as their skin. One's skin was blue. It had green eyes, and had a dress made from pink flower petals. The other had green skin, blue eyes, and a smock made of green tropical leaves. Each had a smile on their face, and they were playfully flying around.

"We are going to take you the rest of the way to Queen Zana and Queen Tania on Fairy Island," the blue one said and flew over to pick Frankie up. The other one flew over to Mikael and picked him up.

The two caterpillars said goodbye to Ava and headed across the ocean to Fairy Island.

They flew across the water, and shortly made their way to their destination. Once they were over the island, they could see an incredible untouched paradise. They approached a clearing, which was surrounded by big, tropical flowers. As they got closer, they could see a rainbow of small, colorful lights dancing across the sky.

"Look at all the fairies!" Mikael exclaimed.

They were headed toward two little chairs made of twigs that were nestled on a rock on top of the clearing. They looked like thrones, and the most beautiful creatures they had ever seen were sitting on them.

They were placed in front of Queen Zana and Queen Tania. Queen Zana looked human, but her skin was light pink. A ring of flowers was on top of her long, blonde hair. Her little eyes were bright blue, and her dress went down to her feet and was made of perfectly placed little flowers sewn to each other. She had multicolor wings and was holding a golden scepter in one of her hands.

Sitting next to her was Queen Tania. She was another beautiful fairy. Her skin was light blue, she had long brown hair and pink eyes. She was wearing a dress exactly like Queen Zana. She also had a ring of flowers around her head, multicolor wings, and a golden scepter in one of her hands.

They sat down in front of the Queens on seats made of twigs, slightly distracted by the lights dancing around them and circling overhead. As the lights approached, their forms became more and more clear as fairies. As the fairies landed, they perched themselves inside the petals of the flowers. One by one, the entire frolic of fairies joined in.

Queen Zana said to Mikael and Frankie, "Welcome, we've been expecting you. This is my wife, Queen Tania."

They were mesmerized by their beauty.

"Hello," Frankie said shyly.

"Nice to meet you," Mikael blushed.

"Have you been told of the final gift to the Shaman?" she asked.

"A Sacred Crystal," Mikael said.

"Yes, a Sacred Crystal and it is inside the Sacred Lotus. We are going to teach you how to retrieve it," Queen Zana said. "One must have a heart of pure love in order to open the Sacred Lotus and obtain the Sacred Crystal. In order to have a heart of pure love, you must forgive all those who have hurt you or rejected you for being different."

"Um, okay," Frankie said reluctantly.

"This isn't going to be easy," Mikael chimed in.

"This will be the hardest gift for you to obtain. By forgiving, you will release all the hurt that is within, and you will transform your heart into pure love. Then you will be able to retrieve the Sacred Crystal."

"We are going to help you forgive by showing you why each one who hurt you acted the way they did," Queen Tania said.

The sun had set, and the sky was dusky. Queen Tania threw fairy dust in the air, and they could see Zak's upbringing play like a movie screen in the air in the form of a hologram. They saw his father treat him the exact same way he had treated Mikael and Frankie in Coconut Grove. They also saw that

his friends were actually scared of Zak,
so they pretended to be just like him. In
actuality, they were really just trying to avoid
the same treatment.

Frankie and Mikael were shocked.

Frankie saw that her parents were treated
poorly by her grandparents and peers. Mikael
saw that all of his caregivers were mistreated
too. They also saw that the seagull needed
glasses and kept trying to eat them because it
thought they were walking french fries.

Frankie looked over at Mikael. "I wasn't
expecting that," she said while crying.

Mikael glanced back, tears on his face too.
"Me either."

"Are you two ready to forgive?" Queen
Zana asked.

"I don't know if I can. My parents were
really mean to me because I wasn't what they
wanted me to me." Frankie said looking down
at the ground.

Queen Zana told her, "They didn't learn

to speak to their inner gardens or have the freedom to be their true selves. They don't love themselves because they were never shown how to. It wasn't right how they treated you, but we hope that knowing the truth will help you let go of the pain they caused you and forgive them."

Frankie nodded, and then she said out loud, "I forgive them for the pain they caused me."

"I am incredibly proud of you," Queen Zana said tenderly. She switched focus to Mikael. "Are you ready to forgive everyone who hurt you?" she asked.

"They were mean to me because they were taught to be that way and didn't have love in their hearts?" Mikael asked.

"Yes," Queen Zana replied.

"Well, I guess that makes more sense as to why I was treated so bad too." Mikael took a deep breath and exhaled. "I forgive everyone for the pain they caused me."

The frolic of fairies let out a cheer. Queen

Zana and Queen Tania stood up and clapped for them relentlessly.

They sat back down and proceeded, "Now, we are going to sing a song of love over you, and we would like you to receive it and take it into your heart. You need to be filled with love in your heart in order for the Sacred Lotus to open up to allow you inside to obtain the Sacred Crystal. If you have anything negative in your heart such as anger, fear, doubt, or disbelief, the Sacred Lotus will not open," Queen Tania said.

Mikael and Frankie sat, listening to the fairies as they started to sing. It sounded like a symphony of angels filling the sky. Soon, all the fairies joined together and sang:

> *Love, love*
> *is the greatest gift.*
> *Love is powerful.*
> *Feel our love.*
> *Let it heal you.*
> *Let it transform you.*

124

As the fairies sang their song of love over them, Frankie and Mikael noticed colored lights shooting from each of the fairies that made it look like a rainbow shining around them. The smell of the garden intensified, and the light of the moon became more vibrant. They felt each word vibrate deep within each of them, causing them to feel an overwhelming sense of acceptance. They immediately cried and embraced each other, letting in the wonderful, healing gift of love from the fairies.

Afterward, Queen Tania stated, "The most powerful weapon on this planet is love, most especially love for oneself. When you do accept that, no other negative word or action will ever harm you again. You are different, not like the other caterpillars, and yet here you are on an epic journey unlike anyone else's on this planet. And why? We believe that you have a unique and wonderful destiny ahead of you and are very special."

When they were finished, they decided to

embark on their journey to the Sacred Lotus. It was in the middle of the island on top of a hill. They gathered their belongings and inched forward, following the dancing lights of the fairies leading the way.

The fairies were flying around them with their multicolor lights illuminating the path to the Sacred Lotus. They all started to sing again, and Mikael and Frankie couldn't help but join:

> *Love, love*
> *is the greatest gift.*
> *Love is powerful.*
> *Feel our love.*
> *Let it heal you.*
> *Let it transform you.*

They arrived at the Sacred Lotus and awaited further instruction.

Queen Tania flew over to speak to them. "Okay," she said urgently, "the Sacred Lotus blooms only when it is completely illuminated by the moon's light and with our song. We are the key to opening it. The minute that you see the moon's light illuminating it entirely, I will drop you inside to grab the Sacred Crystal. It will only stay open for a short time."

"Oh no!" Frankie burst out. "Only for a short time?"

"We must trust and believe in ourselves, Frankie," Mikael said. "If we doubt ourselves, then our hearts won't be full of love, and we won't get the crystal."

The frolic of fairies sang their song of love again, and Queen Tania flew over to Mikael. She grabbed him, picked him up, and flew him over to the Sacred Lotus just as the moon started to fully illuminate it. She dropped him at the perfect moment, just as the flower was opening.

Suddenly they heard, "Squawk, squawk!" Overhead, the seagull appeared. It swooped in and grabbed Mikael the minute Queen Tania dropped him.

Frankie acted quickly, saying, "Hurry, grab

me so I can help," as she motioned to a group of fairies who were flying close to her.

A couple of the fairies swooped in and grabbed Frankie, lifting her up toward the pesky bird. Frankie reached in her satchel, looking desperately for something that could help. She grabbed the rock that Marakata gave her and threw it in the bird's face, hitting it between its eyes. "We are not french fries!" she shouted, annoyed.

Surprised, the bird flew around in a distracted circle, dropping Mikael at the exact same spot that he was before, directly above the Sacred Lotus. Now it was fully open.

Mikael felt himself falling again. Once he landed, he lay there with his eyes closed, unaware that he was inside the blossom.

Then he heard Frankie shouting, "Quick, quick, get the crystal! You don't have much time!"

Mikael opened his eyes, looked around, and he realized he was inside the Sacred Lotus. He opened and closed his eyes in disbelief. He stood in amazement, taking in the beauty with all of his senses. He scrambled to get to the Sacred Crystal in the center. He took one long look at the Sacred Crystal and took the deepest breath he could muster. Then he grabbed it and immediately put it in his satchel.

One of the fairies flew inside the flower, grabbed him, and set him on the ground.

Frankie ran over to Mikael and they embraced. "We did it! We did it!" they cried. They immediately turned to the fairies to thank them for all their help.

"We wouldn't have been able to finish our journey to the Shaman without you," Mikael said.

"It has been my pleasure to assist you both on your journey," Queen Zana said to them. "We'll send for the unicorn to take you to the Shaman in the morning now that you have completed the last task. You two must be exhausted after having such an eventful day."

Frankie's eyes widened. "Wow, unicorns exist too!"

Queen Zana laughed, "I'll show you two where to sleep for the night and will awaken you in the morning when it is time to go to the Shaman."

Chapter 13

The Shaman

The morning arrived, and the two were awoken to complete their journey to the Shaman.

A glorious, white unicorn gracefully bowed its head, and Mikael and Frankie climbed on. Its horn and tail were the color of a rainbow.

Frankie was so excited she asked it, "What's your name?"

Before it had a moment to respond, Mikael nudged her to wave goodbye to the fairies. They thanked the fairies as they readied themselves to head out for their final destination.

Queen Zana and Queen Tania said, "Come visit us again, please."

"We will," they said, waving goodbye to their friends.

"My name is Kiki," the unicorn said. "It is a pleasure to meet you. We are setting out to the Shaman's hut on the tallest mountain peak. Did either of you know that unicorns have a magic ability to just disappear and then reappear where they want to?"

"No!" Frankie said excited.

"Whoa!" Mikael said.

"I am going to count to three, and then we are going to appear on the tallest mountain peak, at the Shaman's hut." The unicorn counted to three, and then they appeared at the Shaman's hut like magic. "Can we do that again?" Frankie asked.

"Not this time. I must go now. You have important things to ask the Shaman." Kiki said goodbye and then disappeared.

They stood there in awe.

The eagle was there to greet them. "I have been expecting you." She ushered them inside her home.

They pulled out the gifts and handed them to the Shaman. The crystal reflected the light of the morning sun, making rainbows dance around them.

Mikael paused, remembering the fairies with a smile on his face. "We had a wish granted from the fountain to find you. We would like to be placed in a new home," he said.

The Shaman didn't respond. Instead, she gave them a long, considering look.

Frankie started to squirm and said, "Shaman, can you say something, please? You're making me uncomfortable just staring at us."

133

The Shaman continued to gaze at them.

"Are we in trouble?" Frankie asked uncomfortably.

After what felt like an eternity, she finally spoke. "The only way someone can possess the Sacred Crystal is if they have a pure heart and are full of love. There hasn't been anyone before you who has been able to bring me this crystal, and believe me, there have been a lot who have tried. Not only that, but for hundreds of years, my family has been keepers of the fountain, and it has not granted a wish to anyone who has asked. Yet it sent you two on a journey to find me."

Frankie and Mikael looked at each other, amazed.

"It must have been able to see that your inner light and capabilities are far more than I imagined. Not only did you find me, but it appears that you have already been on a special journey before arriving here." She paused and inspected the gifts. "I see by the vial containing the Sacred Fire that you were taken to visit King Muno, the keeper of the Sacred Fire. What did the fire teach you?"

"It told Mikael to jump in, and we did it together," Frankie offered. "Then I could hear it, too, and it told us that there isn't anything wrong with us for being different than others. We sat there and let its light burn away the rejection we felt from other caterpillars our age for being different. It also burned away the pain caused by elders and parents for rejecting us and being upset that we are different too."

"And it told us that we are perfect just as we are," Mikael chimed in.

"I see a vial of Sacred Earth from Marakata and the Sacred Garden. What did he teach you?" the Shaman asked.

"We spoke love to his garden. He had me tell pansies that they were beautiful and loved and had Frankie tell a palm tree that it was special and brave," Mikael answered. "Then we closed our eyes and told the same thing to our inner gardens."

"I see a vial of Sacred Water from the Sacred Water Temple. What did you both see when you saw your reflection in the Waterfall of Truth?" the Shaman asked.

"I saw a special and brave butterfly, and Mikael didn't speak for a while after he saw his reflection," Frankie responded.

"I was faced with something that I had known for a while but wasn't ready to express until we went to the Sacred Temple of Wind. While we were there, I was able to express my inner truth and accept myself fully for who I am," Mikael said. "I then showed it to the entire island. I finally felt free and completely myself."

"I told a joke during my performance at the Sacred Temple of Wind," Frankie said. "I wore a hat and bowtie and felt really cool and completely myself too."

"What did Queen Zana, Queen Tania, and the fairies teach you, and how did you obtain the Sacred Crystal from the Sacred Lotus?" the Shaman asked.

"We were taught that we needed to forgive all those who have hurt us," Frankie said. "We also learned that we must love ourselves most of all. Love is the most powerful weapon we can use against any rejection or hurtful thing that happens from now on."

"What did you see at the Waterfall of Truth, Mikael?" the Shaman asked.

Tears welled up in his eyes, and fear swarmed within, paralyzing him. Mikael took a deep breath in and remembered everything he had just been taught. His eyes were closed as he opened his mouth to speak his truth. "Inside, I am female. My inner self is Mikaela, not Mikael."

"I am incredibly proud of you," the Shaman told her. "That isn't an easy thing for you to say. You listened to all the advice that was given on your journey, and you used it to tell the deepest and most beautiful truth about yourself. I can imagine that wasn't easy, but I am here to tell you that I am proud of you for being so incredibly brave to speak your truth."

Mikael—now Mikaela—cried tears of relief.

Frankie looked at her best friend and cried tears of relief for her too.

Frankie said, "I wasn't completely honest. I saw myself marrying a girl butterfly at the Waterfall of Truth."

"Thank you both for speaking your inner truth," the Shaman said. She paused and reflected for a moment. "You two have come to me for a new home, but you are ready for your transformation. You are ready to be butterflies. Mikaela, when you transform you will be entirely female."

"That makes me so happy!" Mikaela answered, crying tears of joy.

The Shaman replied, "You will be able to be your true self too, Frankie. You will be able to marry a girl butterfly."

Frankie smiled.

The Shaman paused again, then looked at them and stated, "You have both been incredibly strong and brave on your journey. Strength is not the absence of weakness; it is overcoming it. Courage is not the absence of fear; it is facing it. You are both special and radiate love and beauty from within because you have learned to love yourselves for your differences, not despite them." She wiped a tear off her beak. "Neither one of you would have been able to achieve this without the other. The greatest journeys in life aren't always meant to be taken alone."

"Yes," Frankie said, "I just wanted to feel accepted, but I didn't realize I already had that with Mikaela. I never would have overcome so many fears, faced so many obstacles, and achieved all of this if you didn't make a wish and urge me to come with you, Mikaela."

Mikaela had a huge smile on her face. "It feels good to be called by the name that feels right to me," she said proudly. "I wouldn't be standing here today if you hadn't helped me get here, Frankie."

They embraced.

"Looks like living with Miss Black was the perfect place for you after all. If you hadn't lived there, you would have never met each other and taken this incredible journey together," the Shaman gently pointed out. "Sometimes we don't fit in where we don't belong. It is designed to help us find the place that we do."

"You're right," Mikaela said. "I am now home within myself, and I love that I am different."

"I am home within myself too," Frankie said with satisfaction.

"One more thing," the Shaman added. "When you two become butterflies, you will need to fly back to Coconut Grove and tell the caregivers you left that you are sorry for leaving."

They agreed.

"All those who hurt you will transform into moths because they have such hate in their hearts. Now it is time to go build your chrysalises. All of the gifts that you have brought me will help you build them." The Shaman emptied the contents of the vials of sacred elements, split them in half, and handed the portions to the two friends. She also gave them each a piece of the crystal to use to build their chrysalises. She reflected for a moment and then looked at Mikaela, "I have watched you struggle to fit in your whole life, but now it brings me great joy to see you accept and love yourself for your differences instead of despite them. When you transition into a butterfly, you will be the most beautiful butterfly who ever lived because of the beauty that radiates within your heart. It will glow from the inside out."

Mikaela smiled.

Frankie and Mikaela built their chrysalises on the Shaman's property, high upon the mountain top overlooking the beautiful landscape of Emerald Island.

Much time passed, but finally, the time came for Frankie and Mikaela to be reborn.

A crowd of their friends who had helped them on their journey gathered to watch them hatch out of their chrysalises.

Mikaela hatched first. She saw her pink glitter scarf lying next to her and immediately put it on. She turned her golden body and looked at her wings. Her eyes brightened. She shone the way the sun glistens on a drop of dew in the morning light of a new day. She spread her wings and started to fly. She felt the exhilaration of being in the air and started to glide. She was free at last. Her golden crystal wings glistened in the sun. The light rays streamed through her wings and caused beautiful little rainbows to appear all over the ground below her. She truly was the most beautiful butterfly who ever lived.

"Mikaela, wait up. How do I work these things?" Frankie had hatched and was trying to catch up. She turned and looked at her body, a bold blue with multicolor wings. "So cool!" she said as she was trying to figure out how to fly. She grabbed her hat, which the Shaman had placed next to her while she was in her chrysalis. She smiled and put it on her head.

"Just start flapping your wings and trust yourself," Mikaela advised while gliding in the air.

Frankie started flapping, and soon was no longer on solid foundation. She was in the air. "I'm off the ground! The view is so much better from up here!" She looked down and saw all of their friends cheering them on. "Look, Mikaela, they came here to see us transform and become butterflies."

Mikaela and Frankie flew around the crowd that had gathered below. "Thank you all for your kindness," Mikaela said. "If it wasn't for all of you, I wouldn't have transformed into a beautiful butterfly." A rainbow appeared on the horizon.

They all cheered. "You're welcome, Mikaela!"

Frankie thanked them too, but got distracted and landed on the elephant.

The crowd let out a giant laugh.

Ava let out a sound like a trumpet from her trunk.

Then Frankie and Mikaela flew up and away, each inspired to chase dreams anew.

When the story was finished, Carlisle looked over at Jasper, who was almost asleep on the couch.

"Grandpa, what happened when they went back to Coconut Grove?" Jasper asked.

"They went back, and Frankie's parents cried and felt horrible for how they treated her. When it came time for them to transform, they became moths because they still didn't have love in their hearts, but they never asked Frankie to take off her beloved hat again."

"What happened to Miss Black?"

"She was so overwhelmed by Mikaela's beauty that she decided to transform, but became a moth because of the years of pain she inflicted to all the poor young caterpillars in her care."

"What about the bullies?"

"Zak and his friends tried to follow the same journey that Mikaela and Frankie set out on, but Zak got eaten by the seagull, and then was barfed back up when it realized that Zak wasn't a french fry. Zak was never the same after that. He never transitioned into a moth nor a butterfly, and was last seen roaming the rainforest, still in search of the Shaman. His sidekicks actually ended up becoming butterflies and became friends with Frankie and Mikaela."

"Grandpa, I want to become a beautiful butterfly like Mikaela," they whispered.

He lovingly looked at his grandchild. "You already are, kiddo."

Jasper replied, "I forgive the kid who pulled my hair and called me mean things today. The things he said aren't true. I am beautiful and kind and there is nothing wrong with me for being different."

Carlisle said, "I am so proud of you for saying that."

"Grandpa, do you think that his family treats him like he did me?"

"I don't know for sure, kiddo, but I can't imagine that he has learned to be that mean on his own."

"I am so lucky that I have you, Grandpa."

They embraced.

Jasper paused for a second and then asked, "Can I start going by my mother's name instead of Jasper?"

Carlisle reached out, gave them another hug, and kissed their forehead. "Absolutely, kiddo. I think she would be honored. I will start calling you Ella."

Ella smiled.

"And starting now, I'm going to volunteer to be the groundskeeper at your school. The place is a mess, and that way, I will always be around if you need me or if you feel scared. I am also going to have a very long talk with the principal and the parents of the kid who said mean things so that you won't have to go through that again. We are going to try to educate them on just how special you are, kiddo, and how it isn't okay to treat you that way."

"Okay, Grandpa. Can I hear the story again?" Ella asked.

Carlisle chuckled. "This time I am going to change the name from Mikaela to Ella. Because you are definitely the most beautiful butterfly who ever lived."

Transformed

Acknowledgments

I would like to thank all of those who have supported and helped me on my own healing journey, without whom I wouldn't have been able to embark on my own inner transformation.

It has been incredibly important to make sure that the content of the book is respectful in every way possible. Special thank you to Ken Sturtz MA, LMHC, for making sure that the content is respectful toward the LGBTQ+ community through the eyes of a counselor. I am incredibly grateful for your generosity and support.

I would like to thank my mentor and friend,

Susan Pullen, for the endless laughs and the wisdom imparted to me on my journey. I am eternally grateful for everything.

I would also like to thank all of my friends who I consider family: Brandi, Kristyn, Leah, and Amber. Without your love and support it wouldn't have been possible.

Special thank you to Brandi Gordon-Bennett for being a best friend and sister. Thank you for taking me in, teaching me what a family truly is, and making me a part of yours.

Kristyn Berkley, thank you for traveling to Bali with me as I started this journey, and also spending hours with me crying and laughing during the rewrites and birth of this book. Your friendship means the world to me, and I am grateful you are part of my chosen family.

Thank you to Enjoli Izidor for the cover design.

A special thank you to all of my LGBTQ+ family for all of your love and support.

About the Author

Amaia Brooke is a member of the LGBTQ+ community and identifies as a lesbian.

Disowned from her family after coming out to them as an adult, she embarked on a healing journey. Digging into the well within helped her realize

that the rejection of her family started during childhood and affected her youth. Growing up she was taught that homosexuality was bad and wrong, and not having a supportive environment created a negative self-image. She decided to use the healing of that experience to write a children's story that offers visibility, love and acceptance for LGBTQ+ youth. She realized how beneficial it would have been to have something like that for herself as a child. While this book highlights themes that affect transgender and lesbian readers, the universal truths are in it for all. She wants to empower those that may be experiencing bullying from peers or rejection from family to know that there is nothing wrong with who they are, and to fiercely love and accept themselves regardless. Amaia currently resides in Seattle, WA surrounded by her incredible chosen family.

Please visit transformed.world.com for more information.

Transformed

CPSIA information can be obtained
at www.ICGtesting.com
Printed in the USA
JSHW021202060919
1367JS00001B/2

9 781733 388207